W9-BNA-359

The Trouble with Northrup

A Trampoline's Highs and Lows

Jimmy Aaron's Best Worst Day of Fifth Grade

THREE COMEDIES

by Jeffrey B. Fuerst

illustrated by Anthony Carpenter and Kevin Kelly

Table of Contents

What is a play?

A play is a story written in script form (words for actors to say and stage directions). The main goal is the script is performed by actors in front of an audience. Some people enjoy reading plays in the same way that they read a story, though the format is different. The events in a play are shown in short sections called scenes. The scenes may be grouped into larger sections called acts. Many plays are divided into two or three acts. Plays consist almost entirely of dialogue—conversation between people.

What is the purpose of a play?

A play shows people in action. The main characters face a conflict or have a problem to solve. The purpose of a play is to let the audience (or reader) connect with the characters in the story and experience their emotions. The audience has a chance to share the characters' success or failure, and to feel the same fear, love, hope, joy, and other emotions that the characters feel as the play develops.

How do you read a play?

Part of the fun of reading a play is getting to know the characters. They are usually described in a section that precedes the play. Pay careful attention to the dialogue. Nearly all of the information about the characters and the plot comes from what the characters say and do. Then note the setting, when and where the story takes place. When reading a play, you need to use your imagination to "see" the settings and actions

Features of a Play

- Plays are written to be performed by live actors, onstage.
- Plays usually have one or more main characters and additional minor characters.
- Plays are told through dialogue and characters' actions.
- The play's plot is based on conflict—a problem for the character to solve or a decision to make.
- Play scripts include stage directions.
- Plays take place in one or more time frames and settings.
- Plays may be divided into scenes or acts.

as described by the playwright. Finally, there are notes to the actors, director, and designers called stage directions. Stage directions are written within parentheses. As you read, you will find it helpful to picture who is talking, who is listening, who is onstage, and who is not.

Who invented plays?

The ancient Greeks performed the earliest plays. They came up with the idea of an actor who speaks and acts, or "plays at" being someone else. These early plays influenced future authors of plays, whom we call playwrights (*wright* means "maker"). Centuries later, one of the world's most famous writers, William Shakespeare, wrote many plays that are still read and performed.

TOOLS
for Readers and Writers

Idiom

An idiom (IH-dee-um) is a phrase or expression that makes language more colorful and interesting. Idioms do not use the literal (exact) meaning of the phrase. Consider these sentences: "Uncle Joe is a wet blanket. He makes us go to bed at 9 P.M." "Wet blanket" means that Joe is no fun. Since idioms are commonly used in conversation and writing, people have come to understand what they mean in a particular culture. Playwrights use idioms to give their characters' dialogue an authentic quality.

Adverbs

Playwrights want readers to identify with their characters and their actions. To accomplish this, they include descriptive language in the form of adverbs. Adverbs describe characters' actions by showing how, where, when, and how often things are done. Good readers look for describing adverbs to get the most out of the play.

Cause-and-Effect Relationships

One way writers explain information is to tell why certain events happen. When they write about an event, they often discuss the causes and effects of those events. Good readers pay attention to what happens and to explanations telling why they happened. Identifying each event as the effect and the reason for it as the cause helps readers better understand the text.

Dramatic Literature

Plays are a type of literature called drama. They go back thousands of years. Dramatic literature falls into two broad categories: comedy or tragedy. A comedy is funny and usually has a happy ending. Plots often revolve around miscommunication and mistaken identity. A tragedy is serious and has an unhappy ending. Tragedies often have a main character with a flaw, such as pride or arrogance, that leads to his or her downfall.

FAMOUS COMEDIES

FAMOUS TRAGEDIES

Movies and TV shows—including situation comedies, animated cartoons, mysteries, adventures, and soap operas—are also forms of dramatic literature. Movies are about 100 years old. Television became popular in the 1950s.

Movies and TV shows use storytelling techniques taken from plays, such as dialogue and action. But there is a big difference in how the stories are told. Movies and TV shows are recorded. Actors often re-do their scenes. Then the scenes are put together in an orderly way. Plays are performed live. The action takes place in real time, so there are no do-overs if someone makes a mistake. Although plays can have a few different scenes and sets, playwrights can't put edits or close-ups in their scripts!

Monologues

A play performed by one character is called a monologue. The word **monologue** comes from the Greek words *monos*, meaning "single, alone," and *logos*, meaning "speech, word." A long speech by one character in a play is also called a monologue.

How to Read a Play

When performing a play, only the dialogue is spoken.

Character names are not spoken.

Dialogue is spoken.

Mac: That's not good.

Yolanda: Sorry!

Jimmy: No, I'm sorry. It was my fault.

Yolanda: Let me help you up.

Jimmy: Thanks, but I can handle it.

Yolanda: Oh, come on! We're in this together. One, two—

Jimmy: —three!

Stage directions are not spoken.

(YOLANDA *helps pull* JIMMY *to his feet. They assume their positions to dance.*)

Yolanda: (*calm, friendly*) Let's try this again. Ready?

Jimmy: One, two—

Instructions to actors are not spoken.

Yolanda: —three!

Jimmy and Yolanda: One, two, three. One, two, three. One—

Mac: Go, Jimmy!

The Trouble with Northrup

Cast of Characters

DOCTOR KLOPPENNOGGIN: A well-known child psychiatrist, age 54.

MOM: A pretty woman with more worry lines than she would like to have, age 40.

DAD: A tall man with longish hair and a faraway expression in his eyes, age 45.

AUNTIE: A large, loud woman in large, loud clothes, age 65, though she will only admit to "39-plus."

GRAMPS: A fit man with a trim mustache, age 70.

NORTHRUP: An average boy, neither thin nor fat, short nor tall, in clothes that are not too trendy or too nerdy, age 12.

Setting

Dr. Kloppennoggin's office, Tuesday afternoon, 4:15 P.M.

(Lights up on DOCTOR KLOPPENNOGGIN's office. It is more like a pleasant living room than an examining room, with a couch, easy chairs, side tables. DOCTOR sits in a rocking chair, writing on a pad. NORTHRUP sits quietly, sullenly, on an ottoman next to DOCTOR. MOM, DAD, and AUNTIE sit nervously on the comfortable furniture; GRAMPS looks out a window. The action begins in the middle of the appointment.)

DOCTOR: I see, I see. And how long has this been going on?

MOM: I started to notice it about . . . three weeks ago.

DAD: Oh, it hasn't been that long. Has it?

AUNTIE: It's been longer if you ask me.

GRAMPS: No one's asking you. Ask the boy.

AUNTIE: That's the problem! He won't talk. If you ask me, Doctor Kloppennoggin, it's because of all the time he spends on that computer-phone thing. Land sakes, you'd think it was sewn to his hand. E-mail this, Instant Message that. Text, text, text. Twitter, twitter, twitter. Tweet, tweet, tweet. Your fingers do all your talking for you nowadays. It's no wonder you forget how to use your voice.

DOCTOR: I can check his vocal cords.

GRAMPS: *(to AUNTIE)* Go back to the twentieth century if you don't like it. *(to DOCTOR)* Move with the times I say. Look at me: I'm in shape **physically** and **mentally**.

MOM: I think it has something to do with his diet, Doctor. All that white flour and white sugar rot the body from the inside out. Those processed foods with their additives and preservatives are not natural. They can't be good for you. I try to get him to eat fresh fruits and vegetables, but he only wants that junk food he sees on TV.

DAD: That's the real problem. TV, VCR, DVD. He spends too much time sitting in front of electronic devices, watching but never doing. You've got to be active, use your hands and your mind, engage your heart and soul. Make something with your life and you'll have something to say for yourself.

9

GRAMPS: I agree that the boy needs to get outside more. Fresh air, exercise. Get the muscles moving, blood pumping. That'll knock the cobwebs off the brain cells and get the tongue wagging.

DOCTOR: I can give you the name of a personal trainer who is also a nutritionist and an art therapist.

AUNTIE: Bish, bosh! He needs more human interaction.

MOM: A healthy diet with whole grains.

DAD: A creative outlet for personal expression.

GRAMPS: A strict workout regimen.

(The conversation becomes increasingly heated. MOM, DAD, AUNTIE, and GRAMPS are arguing among themselves. NORTHRUP shakes his head while DOCTOR takes notes.)

AUNTIE: Meaningful conversation, I tell you.

MOM: Greens, greens, greens.

DAD: Self-actualization.

GRAMPS: Exercise.

AUNTIE: Face time!

MOM: Roughage!

DAD: A hobby!

GRAMPS: Sweat!

AUNTIE, MOM, DAD, and GRAMPS: *(to one another)* You don't know what you're talking about. You're wrong and I'm right. *(to* DOCTOR*)* Tell them to listen to me. Don't you see that I know what's the trouble with Northrup? *(*DOCTOR *looks at each of them, then ruefully at* NORTHRUP.*)*

NORTHRUP: Quiet! Quiet, all of you! Mom, Dad, Auntie, Gramps— I love you all. I care about each of you and I know you truly care about me. But I don't need more face time, more roughage, a hobby, or exercise. I need you all to be quiet more **often**. I stopped talking because I can **never** get a word in edgewise!
*(*MOM, DAD, AUNTIE, GRAMPS *are taken aback, look at* NORTHRUP, *then at one another. They each give* NORTHRUP *a hug, and then they embrace in a group hug, which breaks apart as* DOCTOR *happily looks on.*)*

MOM: I can be quiet, sweetie.

GRAMPS: You won't hear a peep out of me from here on in.

DAD: Take all the space you need, son.

AUNTIE: You want Auntie to shut up, Auntie shuts up.

MOM: Quiet as a mouse, that's me.

GRAMPS: Zip it right up.

DAD: You'll be able to hear a pin drop around me.

AUNTIE: Just say the word and my lips are sealed. *(pause)* Go ahead, say it.

MOM, DAD, AUNTIE, and GRAMPS: Say it! Say it! *(*NORTHRUP *looks at them all, sighs, then looks at* DOCTOR, *who looks concerned again.*)*

NORTHRUP: Next Tuesday at the same time?

DOCTOR: It's **already** in my appointment book.
(LIGHTS OUT)

A Trampoline's Highs and Lows

Cast of Characters

TRAMPOLINE: A philosophical, commercial-sized trampoline; the kind found in public amusement parks.

CANNONBALL JONES: An eight-year-old ball of energy with a devilish smile who is built like a fire hydrant.

Setting

Uncle Ed's Old-Fashioned Fun-O-Rama,
one Saturday afternoon in summer.

*(Lights up on a **gaily** decorated, though aging, outdoor amusement park. It is a mild summer afternoon. The place is bustling with families and children. "Gay Nineties"—1890s!—songs such as "Sidewalks of New York" and "Daisy Bell (A Bicycle Built for Two)" play in the background. Downstage center is a trampoline, whether an actual prop or cardboard representation. The actor playing TRAMPOLINE stands **nearby**.)*

TRAMPOLINE: As you can imagine, my life as a trampoline is filled with ups and downs. On the up side, there is no greater joy than knowing that I make so many people happy, especially kids, when they're bouncing on me. What giggles! What chuckles! What guffaws! To me, there is no better sound than that of wild, gleeful laughter . . . except, possibly, those moments of silent contentment that fill the spaces between the jumps and laughs. Yes, everyone loves a trampoline, and those times, it is good to be me. Of course, as the laws of gravity tell us, what goes up must come down. And after every boy, girl, teenager, man, woman, and occasional dog who jumps on me heads skyward, up, up, up . . . they fall back down, down, down on me with a forceful "Whap!" *(whining)* It hurts when they land that hard! *(composed)* Okay, I know what you're thinking. If I couldn't take all the pounding, then I should have become a seesaw; or, if I were such a lightweight, I should have done like my cousin Rollo and become one of those inflatable jumping houses at birthday parties for four-year-olds. It's not that. I know that banging down onto my surface is part of what it means to be a trampoline. But people, when you climb on me, can't you show some compassion and just land lightly on your toes? *(pauses, becomes alarmed)* Oh no! Not him! Not Cannonball Jones. Please pass by me. Please pass by me. (CANNONBALL JONES *climbs onto* TRAMPOLINE *and starts jumping, laughing maniacally.*)

TRAMPOLINE: Here we go . . . Ouch! Ow! Ew! OWWWW! Not another knee-drop! OH!!! *(in a shaky voice, indicating he is being bounced on)* Oh well. I'll bounce back! After all, I'm a trampoline. (CANNONBALL JONES *giggles.*)

TRAMPOLINE: Ow! Ouch! Ew!

(LIGHTS FADE TO BLACK)

Analyze the Characters and Plot

Answer the following questions about the play *The Trouble with Northrup*.

- Who are the characters in the play?
- Where does the play take place?
- What is the main problem in the play?
- Is the problem resolved?
- What happens at the end of the play?

Focus on Comprehension: Cause-and-Effect Relationships

- What does Auntie think is causing Northrup's problem?
- Why did Northrup stop talking?
- Trampoline did not want Cannonball Jones to jump on him. Why not?

Focus on

ANTHROPOMORPHISM

Have you read any of Aesop's fables? If so, then you have probably read about animal characters with human characteristics. Giving human qualities to animals or objects is a literary technique called anthropomorphism. The word comes from two Greek words, *anthropos*, which means "human being," and *morphe*, which means "shape." Winnie the Pooh, Woody in *Toy Story*, and the Magic Carpet in *Aladdin* are examples of anthropomorphism. Who is the anthropomorphic character in "A Trampoline's Highs and Lows"? How is this character like a human?

Analyze the Tools Writers Use: Idioms

- What does Auntie mean on page 9 when she says, "Your fingers do all your talking for you nowadays"?
- On page 10, Gramps says that fresh air and exercise will "knock the cobwebs off the brain cells and get the tongue wagging." Do we really have cobwebs in our brains? Do our tongues really wag? What does the author mean by these words?
- Northrup says he can't "get a word in edgewise." (page 11) What did he mean when he said that?
- Dad tells Northrup to take all the space he needs. (page 11) How much space does a person need? Does this mean that Northrup is an overweight child?
- On page 13, Trampoline says, "If I were such a lightweight." What does a lightweight look like? Is it a weight with lightbulbs on it? Or does this idiom mean something else?

Focus on Words: Adverbs

Adverbs are words that describe action. They give additional information about how, when, and where something happens. Make a chart like the one below. Read each adverb and decide what type of adverb it is. Place an X in the correct place on the chart.

Page	Adverb	Adverbs Telling How	Adverbs Telling When	Adverbs Telling Where
9	physically			
9	mentally			
11	often			
11	never			
11	already			
12	gaily			
12	nearby			

Jimmy Aaron's Best Worst Day of Fifth Grade

Cast of Characters

Brief descriptions help readers picture the characters in their mind's eye as the playwright did.

JIMMY AARON: An athletic boy with sandy hair and freckles, short for his age, age 11.

MAC SHIMAZAKI: A roundish boy, with mischief barely concealed in his perpetual half-smile, age 10.

YOLANDA ALOU: A tall, lanky, long-haired girl, reserved until you get to know her, age 11.

COACH JOHNSON: An ex-Marine gone soft in the belly but still a tough drill sergeant at heart, middle-aged.

Setting

The play is purposely set in the past. The playwright is challenging readers to consider how they might handle the same problem, if it happened to them today.

The play takes place on a Thursday afternoon and Friday morning in May 1967.

Scene 1: Jimmy's room.

Scene 2: The gym at Millard Fillmore Elementary School.

The setting (below) is based on a designer's sketch (right).

Scene 1

(Lights up on a boy's bedroom. The walls are covered with posters of famous baseball players of the day. The bookshelves are filled with model airplanes. The floor is littered with dirty clothes. A blue suit is laid out nicely on his bed. JIMMY AARON stands in front of a mirror practicing tying a tie. He becomes increasingly frustrated at his failures. MAC SHIMAZAKI sits in a chair at a desk, gently flipping up/playing catch with a signed baseball. He wears a prominent bandage around his shoeless left ankle. A pair of crutches is nearby.)

In the first stage direction, the playwright describes the setting in more detail and places the characters in the scene. This helps readers get the feel of who the characters are, and eases them into the world of the play.

MAC: The long, fat part goes around the short skinny part, then up through the hole at the top and into the loop. Then you hold down the short end, pull down the long end until it is tight. Then you slowly wiggle the knot up.

JIMMY: Until it chokes my head off! ARGH! I hate ties. I hate button shirts that have collars. I hate having to wear an itchy suit. I hate having to wear shoes that hurt my feet. And most of all, I hate, Hate, HATE **tomorrow**. It's the absolute worst day of fifth grade.

MAC: You saw it coming, man. But you didn't plan ahead, like me.

JIMMY: (*sighs*) I don't have the advantage of an older brother to steer me clear of disasters.

MAC: True. Yoshi gave me the idea of the ankle bandage. But I was the one who faked the skateboard "accident" in which I "sprained" my ankle.

(*MAC bounces up from the chair, evidently not injured. He pretends to be skateboarding then pretends to hit a bump and falls to the ground. He gets ups, now mock-howling in pain. Then he does a little tap-dance, laughs, and sits down.*)

Plays are written in script format. The dialogue is spoken aloud by actors. The character's name comes first, so it is clear who is to speak. Sometimes the playwright includes a stage direction in parentheses after the character's name. These stage directions may suggest the character's emotional state, such as "(sighs)".

18

MAC: You know, I have another crutch at home. It's not too late for you to have an "accident."

JIMMY: I guess I could, but then I'd have to miss the game on Saturday. Coach needs me to pitch. I don't want to let the team down, and it wouldn't feel right if I had a miraculous recovery.

MAC: You're right. The team needs you. Not like me. I'm O-for-April. Besides, getting around school on these crutches is a pain. And for the past three days everyone has been bugging me with the same question: "What happened to you?" So I had to tell them the same story over and over. It's a lot of work just to be in position to miss gym class tomorrow.

JIMMY: Don't remind me. And put down that ball. It was signed by Mickey Mays.

MAC: Okay! Gee, you sure are touchy about this ball. (*pauses*) Yep. It was embarrassing to tell people about my wipeout. But not as embarrassing as it will be to have to dance *with girls* in gym class.

> This line of dialogue sets up a key plot point that will occur in Scene 2. It also reveals a lot about Jimmy's character.

The playwright introduces the main character's problem. Having to get dressed up in a suit and a tie is bad enough, but to do it to dance with girls in gym class is even worse.

Jimmy: I said don't remind me! Ballroom Dancing Day is the worst day of fifth grade. And I've got it worse than everyone else.

Mac: Why?

Jimmy: My dumb last name. Aaron. It starts with an "A." No, it starts with two As! **Alphabetically**, I'm the first boy in the class. I'll be laughed at the loudest and the longest.

Mac: True. I didn't think of that; then again, I didn't have to.

Jimmy: What's worse, Coach Johnson pairs us up alphabetically. That means I'll have to dance with Emily Alter. Not only is she a girl, but she is a *girlie girl*! She wears dresses every day, and ribbons in her hair. She'll probably wear lipstick tomorrow, and smelly old perfume. And I know, I just know, that when we do that stupid waltzy thing they are making us do, she'll squeeze my hand. Gross!

Mac: It could be worse.

Jimmy: Not for you, even if you hadn't figured out a way to get out of this misery. You would have gotten to dance with Sami Saunders. For a girl, she's not bad.

Mac's long speech is an example of a monologue.

Mac: That's true, too. She has a pet rat. She can win your team back in dodgeball. And she knows her way around a burp. I saw her chug a whole can of soda last summer. When she was done, she got this look on her face where her eyebrows were smiling. Then she opened her mouth wide, like a frog about to eat a dragonfly. Then that Sami let out a belch. It wasn't anything fancy like burping the musical scale. Just one long note B-R-A-A-P! B-flat, I think. Very classy.

JIMMY: My point exactly. Dancing with Sami Saunders wouldn't be so bad. She'd certainly have the decency to not squeeze a guy's hand, like Emily Alter.

MAC: You don't have to worry about that.

JIMMY: Sure I do.

MAC: Not anymore. You're not dancing with Emily.

JIMMY: Why not? Did she sprain her ankle for real?

MAC: No. Alphabetically, Emily Alter is no longer the first girl. That new girl who moved here from Mexico is. Yolanda Alou.

JIMMY: You mean that new girl with the long, black hair? The one who is really, really *tall*?

MAC: That's the one.

JIMMY: (*shaking his head*) The worst day of fifth grade just got worse!

(*Lights fade as* JIMMY *pulls up the tie so it is above his head, like a noose.*)

> The playwright makes the main character's problem even worse.
>
> The playwright ends the scene at a dramatic high point, or crisis, that will make the audience want to know what happens next.

> The playwright suggests how lighting can be used to increase the sense of drama. A slow fading away of light lets the reader/audience observe Jimmy's anguish at what will happen to him the next day.

Scene 2

The playwright sets the next scene in a new place, on a new day. He describes this setting in detail and introduces new characters—including the dreaded Yolanda Alou. Think about what the last sentence tells the reader about Yolanda, and why the playwright included it.

(Lights up on a school gymnasium. Upstage center is a basketball hoop. Stage right is a lineup of unhappy, freshly scrubbed boys dressed in nice clothes. These "boys" should be indicated by life-size cutouts or as a wall mural. MAC sits in a chair, his "sprained" ankle up on another chair. JIMMY stands next to him. JIMMY is wearing his white shirt, tie, blue suit, and dress shoes. He also wears a hangdog expression. Along the stage left wall is a lineup of girls, some happy, some less happy, also cutouts, except for YOLANDA ALOU. She wears a dress but looks uncomfortable in it. She pulls and tugs at it.)

MAC: Breathe in, breathe out, buddy. Relax. Remember, dancing is just like walking . . . in a circle. One, two, three. Take it one step at a time and we'll be out of there in no time.

JIMMY: We? It's only me out there, alone, making a fool of himself in front of everyone. You'll be sitting back here with this pack of hyenas.

MAC: True. But I won't be laughing. And I will be out there with you, in spirit. Besides, you won't be alone. Yolanda will be with you. (*He suppresses a snicker.*) You can't miss her. She's the one who has to duck her head or she'll hit the rim.

The playwright reminds the reader of Jimmy's problem.

JIMMY: Stop it or I'll break your ankle for real.

MAC: Sorry. Look on the bright side—she's not wearing high heels like a lot of the girls.

JIMMY: She's still at least five-foot-three.

MAC: And you're at least four-eight.

JIMMY: Four-eight and a half!

(*MUSIC now plays from an old-fashioned 33.3 rpm record player; it is a crackly, worn recording of Johann Strauss's "Blue Danube Waltz."*)

The playwright includes details such as the music playing during a scene.

COACH: **First** up is Aaron and Alou! Let's see you strut your stuff.

(*JIMMY and YOLANDA head toward center stage at the same slow pace. Both are repeatedly counting "One, two, three" and get lost in their absentminded counting of dance steps. They don't notice each other, and they bang into each other.*)

JIMMY and YOLANDA: One, two, three. One, two, three—Oh!

Jimmy's fear has come true. He is being laughed at for dancing clumsily with a girl who is a lot taller than he is.

> (JIMMY *falls down. Laughter explodes from both sides of the gym.*)

MAC: That's not good.

YOLANDA: Sorry!

JIMMY: No, I'm sorry. It was my fault.

YOLANDA: Let me help you up.

> JIMMY: Thanks, but I can handle it.
>
> YOLANDA: Oh, come on! We're in this together. One, two—
>
> JIMMY: —three!
>
> (YOLANDA *helps pull* JIMMY *to his feet. They assume their positions to dance.*)
>
> YOLANDA: (*calm, friendly*) Let's try this again. Ready?

Yolanda is nice toward Jimmy. She is not going to make his problem worse.

JIMMY: One, two—

YOLANDA: —three!

JIMMY and Yolanda: One, two, three. One, two, three. One—

MAC: Go, Jimmy!

COACH: (*to* MAC) That's enough out of you, Mr. Shimazaki.

MAC: Yes, sir.

YOLANDA: Hey! We're dancing.

JIMMY: Um . . . yeah.

YOLANDA: If only we could stop those *hienas*.

JIMMY: Huh?

YOLANDA: *Hienas.* That means "hyenas" in Spanish.

JIMMY: Yeah, them . . . The only way to shut them up is to nail this dancing thing. You know, if I didn't have to wear this stupid suit—

YOLANDA: Or this silly dress.

JIMMY and YOLANDA: And these shoes that hurt my feet.

(*They pause, look at each other, and laugh. JIMMY relaxes for the first time. They dance some more. The sideline laughter subsides.*)

This single word of dialogue—*hienas*—shows that Yolanda isn't so different from Jimmy.

In this exchange of dialogue, the playwright shows that Jimmy has found an ally, not an enemy.

In a play, what is *not* said can be as important as what *is* said. In this stage direction, the playwright tells how the actors can perform this key moment.

YOLANDA: You look nice in your tie.

JIMMY: Maybe. But it's so tight around my neck that I'll have to be fed **intravenously** from now on. Um, your dress is nice. It's got a lot of . . .

YOLANDA: Stupid girlie-girl frilly things?

JIMMY: Well, I wasn't going to say that, but, um, yeah.

The playwright develops the story in a surprising way: Jimmy and Yolanda have a lot in common. They both dislike getting dressed up and admire Mickey Mays.

YOLANDA: I hate it. My mother made me wear it. She said, "You'll look like a young lady."

JIMMY: That's what my mom said, too. Except she said "gentleman."

YOLANDA: I much prefer my jeans and my Mickey Mays jersey.

JIMMY: Really? You have a Mickey Mays jersey? I do, too. He's my favorite player.

YOLANDA: He's good, all right. Especially now that he doesn't strike out so much.

JIMMY: I have an autographed baseball.

YOLANDA: Cool! I have a couple of those, too.

JIMMY: A couple?

The playwright puts the most dramatic moment toward the end. This moment is called the climax.

YOLANDA: I have a lot of Mickey Mays signed stuff. Bats, gloves. He brings me stuff whenever he visits.

JIMMY: What?

YOLANDA: Whenever Mickey is in town, he comes to see my dad. They played together in the winter leagues, in Mexico. Mickey was about nineteen then and my dad was doing more coaching than playing. But he showed Mickey how to hit the curve. Three batting titles and two home run crowns later, he still says it's because of what my dad taught him.

JIMMY: Wow . . . Wow, wow, wow.

(The MUSIC ends. They stop dancing. JIMMY looks in awe at YOLANDA, still holding her hands in dance position.)

COACH: What an excellent beginning to Ballroom Dancing Day. Thank you, Jimmy and Yolanda.

JIMMY: *(dreamily)* You know Mickey Mays. Wow.

YOLANDA: He's teaching me to switch hit. You know, if you ever decide to let go of my hand, you should come over some time when he's around. I'm sure he'd give you some pointers, too.

(JIMMY lets go of YOLANDA's hand and goes back to the boys' side.)

JIMMY: Wow. That Yolanda is totally cool.

MAC: For a girl.

JIMMY: For anyone!

COACH: **Next** up is Biancullo and Bombassa.

(The MUSIC starts up again then fades out as the LIGHTS FADE TO BLACK.)

The main character discovers that dancing with a girl is not the worst thing that could happen. In fact, Jimmy has grown as a person. He learns that girls are people boys might actually be friends with.

Analyze the Characters and Plot

- Who are the characters in the play?
- Where does the play take place?
- What is the main problem in the play?
- How is the problem resolved?

Focus on Comprehension: Cause-and-Effect Relationships

- Jimmy will not fake an accident to get out of dancing. Why not?
- Why does Jimmy fall down?
- Mickey Mays is a better ballplayer now. Why?

Analyze the Tools Writers Use: Idioms

- On page 19, Mac says it is embarrassing to tell people about his wipeout. What is a wipeout?
- On page 23, Jimmy says that Mac will be sitting with a pack of hyenas. Will Mac really be sitting with animals? What does the playwright mean by this?
- Will Jimmy have to be fed intravenously? (page 26) What does he mean by saying this?

Focus on Words: Adverbs

Adverbs are words that describe action. They give additional information about how, when, and where something happens. Make a chart like the one below. Read each adverb and decide what type of adverb it is. Place an X in the correct place on the chart.

Page	Adverb	Adverbs Telling How	Adverbs Telling When	Adverbs Telling Where
18	tomorrow			
20	alphabetically			
23	first			
26	intravenously			
27	next			

How does an author write a

PLAY?

Reread "Jimmy Aaron's Best Worst Day of Fifth Grade" and think about what the playwright did to write this play. How did he develop the characters? The story line? How can you, as a playwright, develop your own play?

1. Decide on a Problem and Conflict

A play is often about a special day. It can be an ordinary day, but something important occurs that influences the life of the main character. The special event in this play is Ballroom Dancing Day. The problem is that Jimmy Aaron will be the first boy in his fifth-grade class to dance with a girl—and first to risk being loudly laughed at. His conflict is with himself: Should he do what his friend Mac did and get out of dancing by faking an injury? If he does, he will not be able to play in a baseball game and will let his team down.

2. Brainstorm Characters

Playwrights ask these questions:
- Who is the main character in my play? What is he or she like? What problem does my main character have?
- Who will help in the play? What is he or she like?
- What other characters will be important to my story? How will these characters help solve the main character's problem?

Character	Traits
Jimmy	respectful; conscientious; determined
Mac	scheming; creative; a good friend
Yolanda	confident; athletic; cool; kind; friendly

3. Brainstorm Setting and Plot

Playwrights ask these questions:
- Where and when does my play take place?
- How will I describe the setting(s)?
- What is the problem of the play?
- What events happen?
- How does the play end?

Setting	Jimmy's bedroom; the elementary school gym
Problem of the Story	Jimmy is worried that Ballroom Dancing Day will be the worst day of his life.
Story Events	1. Jimmy complains to Mac about having to get dressed up for the next day's terrible event: Ballroom Dancing Day (where boys have to dance with girls!). 2. Mac suggests that Jimmy fake an injury, as he did. 3. Jimmy decides he won't do that because then he'd have to take the lie into the weekend and miss an important baseball game. 4. Jimmy, who is short, learns that he will be dancing with a new girl in school, who is very tall. 5. During gym the next day, Jimmy *is* laughed at just as he feared while dancing with Yolanda, the tall girl.
Solution to the Problem	Jimmy and Yolanda hit it off. They survive the dancing and find out they have common interests. Instead of Ballroom Dancing Day being the worst day ever, it turns out to be one of Jimmy's best. (He realizes boys can be friends with girls, especially one who likes baseball as much as he does *and* can introduce him to his favorite player.)

Glossary

alphabetically   (al-fuh-BEH-tih-klee) in the same order as the letters in the alphabet (page 20)

already   (aul-REH-dee) prior to the present time (page 11)

first   (FERST) before all others in time or place (page 23)

gaily   (GAY-lee) in a bright, lively, or cheery manner (page 12)

intravenously   (in-truh-VEE-nus-lee) within or into a vein or veins (page 26)

mentally   (MEN-tuh-lee) as relates to the mind (page 9)

nearby   (neer-BY) close to; not far away (page 12)

never   (NEH-ver) not ever; at no time (page 11)

next   (NEKST) immediately after (page 27)

often   (AU-fen) frequently (page 11)

physically   (FIH-zih-klee) as relates to the body (page 9)

tomorrow   (tuh-MOR-oh) the day after today (page 18)